D🐾NUT

LEADS the TEAM

SkyLight Books

Tandem Light Press
950 Herrington Rd.
Suite C128
Lawrenceville, GA 30044

Tandem Light Press paperback edition 2018

ISBN: 978-1-7328308-4-4
Library of Congress Control Number: 2018964319

PRINTED IN THE UNITED STATES OF AMERICA

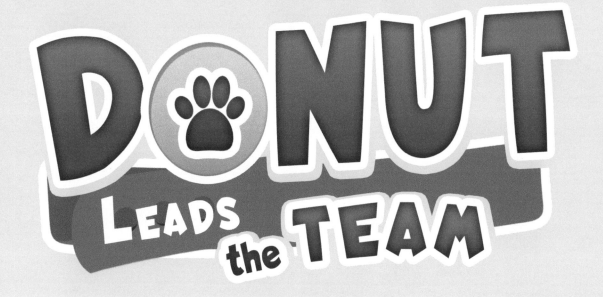

DONUT
LEADS the TEAM

WRITTEN BY

STACY ROBERTS

ILLUSTRATED BY

KAVIYA PUGAZHENDI

Dedication

This book is dedicated to the amazing leaders in our schools, churches, homes, and communities. Thank God for you and everything you do.

It was a sunny day at Poochton Elementary School and a beautiful day to have class outside. The Poochton Pups in Ms. Sunshine's class were excited about the new garden they were about to plant for their class project. Everyone headed outside with their shovels, fertilizer, water pails, and seedlings.

As they walked to their section of the school garden, Ms. Sunshine chose to make Donut the leader of the class project.

"Donut, I believe it's your turn to take the lead for our garden project," said Ms. Sunshine. Donut was thrilled. She had been waiting for her turn to lead a project and wanted to show Ms. Sunshine that she could be a good leader.

When the class reached the garden, Donut began to take charge.

"Roscoe and MiMi, go get the shovels! Charlie and Bill, you can grab water pails. Boomer. Boomer! Grab the seedlings!" Donut yelled.

The class didn't move right away. Donut was usually very kind and didn't talk to them that way.

Slowly Boomer moved to go get the seedlings and the other classmates began to get the other supplies needed to plant their garden.

Mimi and Roscoe found a spot and began to dig holes to plant the seedlings. Just as Mimi was about to dig in the soil again, Donut walked up to her and snatched her shovel.

"Hey! Donut that was my job!" MiMi yelled.

"You weren't digging it right!" Donut yelled back.

Mimi was getting angry. "You just could have told me. You don't have to snatch and take my job." Donut ignored Mimi and continued to dig holes with Roscoe.

Donut looked up to see Charlie and Bill filling the water pails with water from the garden hose. She tossed down Mimi's shovel and ran over to the boys.

Bill was almost finished filling up the last water pail when Donut snatched it, making a big mess. Water splashed everywhere and the three pups were soaked.

"Um, Donut. Why did you do that?" Charlie asked.

"You were filling up the pails with too much water," Donut said. The boys could tell she was upset.

"Why didn't you just say that, Donut?" Bill asked.

Donut didn't answer. She was getting annoyed with her classmates. "I'm the leader today and no one is listening to me," she thought.

She looked back over to Mimi and Roscoe and saw that Boomer was moving the seedlings close to the holes. *Good*, she thought. *At least Boomer is listening today*.

Donut saw the big heavy bag of fertilizer and decided to move it to the holes where the seedlings would be planted. She knew the bag was heavy and that she should ask for help, but she was the leader and needed to show her class that she could move the bag on her own.

Donut grabbed the corner of the bag and began to drag it. It was very heavy but Donut wanted to move by herself. Boomer looked up and saw that Donut needed help.

"Wait, Donut! We can help you with that," Boomer called out. Donut continued to pull the heavy bag.

"I got it!" Donut yelled.

Ms. Sunshine saw Donut having a hard time with the fertilizer. "Donut, wait. Let Roscoe or Boomer help," she said.

"I got it!" Donut said in a strained voice.

Mimi looked at Donut and the bag of fertilizer. It was starting to rip open where Donut was holding it. "Donut stop! The bag is ripping," Mimi cried out.

Donut was straining and sweating. "I said I...whoa!" Donut screamed as she fell to the ground. The bag ripped open and fertilizer flew everywhere! Donut and Ms. Sunshine were covered in the smelly stuff. Everyone froze as Donut slowly stood and looked at her friends and teacher.

The entire playground was quiet and then everyone heard it. A little laugh was coming from Charlie and it slowly got louder and louder. He couldn't help it and his laughter quickly spread to the other pups. First Boomer started, then Roscoe and Mimi. Finally Bill, Donut, and Ms. Sunshine joined in.

Donut felt bad. She was so excited that she was chosen to lead the class project that she forgot that she had a team to help her. Good class leaders knew how to speak to and work with their team to get a job done. She realized hadn't been the best leader that day.

"Are you alright, Donut?' asked Ms. Sunshine.

"I'm sorry everyone. I shouldn't have treated you the way I did and I should have asked for help," she said quietly.

"It's okay, Donut. That's what we're here for. We want to help you. I'm going to go find some paper towels for you and Ms. Sunshine," Mimi said as she headed inside.

"Come on Donut. Let's plant our garden. You can spread the fertilizer since you already smell like it," Boomer said with a laugh.

Ms. Sunshine's class worked together with Donut leading the way and by the time Mimi came back outside with the paper towels, they had planted some of the seedlings, covered them in fertilizer, and watered the garden.

"Wow. That was fast!" Mimi said as she reached the garden area.

Donut looked at everyone and smiled. She was happy she learned a lesson in teamwork and being a good leader that afternoon.

Their seedlings were planted and with the help of her entire class, they had a beautiful garden in no time. Donut now understood that she and her class worked better, together.

About the Author

Stacy Roberts currently resides in Evans, Georgia, where she enjoys spending time with her family and working with organizations to create and cultivate healthy workplace environments.

She is the Founder and President of SMR Leadership Solutions, LLC, also located in Evans, Georgia. She earned her executive coaching certification from the International Coaching Federation approved organization, Academy of Creative Coaching. In addition to her coaching certification, she also has obtained her bachelor's degree in Marketing from Augusta University and her master's degree in Human Resources from Liberty University. She is currently pursuing her Doctor of Business Administration in Human Resources from Liberty University.

Stacy loves to work with young people. I addition to writing children's books, she works with the youth at her church, New Life Worship Center in Hephzibah, Georgia, where she is also a licensed minister.

Stacy is also the author of the Boomer, Be Nice and Roscoe's Rescue. Her books help teach key skills and valuable lessons to young children. She believes that leadership skills can be developed at a young age and help children develop into wholesome and successful adults.

CPSIA information can be obtained
at www.ICGtesting.com
Printed in the USA
BVHW022249201118
533651BV00010B/26/P

* 9 7 8 1 7 3 2 8 3 0 8 4 4 *